VOX ANGELICA

VOX ANGELICA

poems by Timothy Liu

alicejamesbooks
farmington, maine 04938

The poems in this book first appeared in the following publications:
Antioch Review: His Body Like Christ Passed In And Out Of My Life.
Caliban: On A Hill At Night In A Chair Under Stars, Patience,
    Sodom And Gomorrah.
Cimarron Review: Volunteers At The AIDS Foundation.
Indiana Review: SFO/HIV/JFK.
Kenyon Review: 911, Pornography.
The New Republic: Awaiting Translation, Last Christmas.
North American Review: Mama.
Parnassus: From Xian 1 & 2.
Pequod: Passion, The Tree That Knowledge Is.
The Quarterly: Aphrodite As I Know Her, Ariel Singing, Carcass,
    The City, Consolation, The Gates Of Hell, The Heat,
    Indian Summer, The Kore, Labyrinth, Leaving The Universe,
    Neither Moth Nor Rust, She Sings In All Her Seasons.
Quarterly West: From Xian 3 & 4.
River Styx: A Room Without Doors, Separation.
Southwest Review: More Than Half The Leaves Already Down.
Western Humanities Review: Canker, Eros Apteros, The Storm,
    Walking In A World Where We Are Sometimes Loved.
Wisconsin Review: The Other Language.

I would like to thank Richard Howard, Linda Gregg and Gordon Lish for
their friendship and support. And of course, I am indebted to Stewart James
whose meticulous attention and *disturbances in attention* have guided me toward
the true source from which poetry springs.

Library of Congress Cataloging-in-Publication Data
Liu, Timothy
Vox Angelica
I. Title
PS3562.I799V6   1992   811'—dc20   92-10732   CIP
ISBN 0-914086-97-9

Book Design by Lisa Benham
Cover Painting: *Vox Angelica* (detail) by Max Ernst
            Private Collection, New York

*Alice James Books gratefully acknowledges support from the National Endowment
for the Arts and from the Massachusetts Cultural Council, a state agency whose funds
are recommended by the Governor and appropriated by the State Legislature.*

Alice James Books are published by the Alice James Cooperative, Inc.
Alice James Books, 98 Main Street, Farmington, ME 04938

THIRD PRINTING

FOR WILLIAM DAVIS GUNTER JR.

Every man who longs indefatigably for his country, who is distracted from his desire neither by Calypso nor by the Sirens, will suddenly find that he is there.

SIMONE WEIL

CONTENTS

III

FOREWORD

The elements which can be isolated, analyzed, identified in a speculative reading of these poems— a reading which surmises that the new poet writes more than a luckily efficient poem here, a laudably effective poem there, writes instead a consistent and therefore recoverable gist of experience; writes *poetry* rather than poems merely—such elements in Timothy Liu's work are cognate to those we remember and recognize in the sorrowing Catholic poets who prompted adherence and even a sort of addiction a hundred years ago, Coventry Patmore and Francis Thompson. Among such elements are an atmosphere of repugned profanation, a transfiguring (though volatile) faith, and the victimage of erotic despair, along with emblems of a flagrant, an almost predatory purity operating upon us by sacramental negotiations and not to be aspired to *inherently* by a nature so wrecked and warped as ours. It is the particular combination of such elements, one might almost say their direction, which differentiates Timothy Liu from these fin-de-siècle poets (whom I venture he has not much read, and with whom I would include the less doctrinal, and probably just as alien early Claudel), though so sensational are the events and evidences of Liu's poems that I think it expedient to be reminded that such pangs, and such raptures, have been recognizably suffered in poetry, however genteel, however enveloped in a late-Victorian or high symbolist diction of inflammable gas.

The differentiating mixture, the altered direction in this new poet (if I have rightly identified the elements) is perhaps accounted for by his luxuriant circumstance as a young Asian of conflicted Christian (Mormon) faith, the conflict deriving in part from a flagitious homosexuality and in part from an alienated maternal bond—indeed an acknowledged bondage to what we have learned to call the Devouring Mother. In Liu's text the ascent, the ecstatic apprehension of the divine (he is a religious poet, there are no two ways about it, though perhaps there are twenty) can be effected only by a demonic insistence upon abjection, upon the descent ("that swan song in our throats / a falling cloud of ash"). He shrives himself, and his poems show the marks of the lash—they *are* the lash—by an indulgence of such forbidden graces as negation, sacrifice, denial and constraint ("The wings are no longer there / to lift this god out of time"). Where the earlier poets with whom he has an affinity are elevated by their hounding faith, Liu is pulled down ("It was belief that kept us at each other's throats"). And his vision is naturalized to a degree that would astonish his predecessors, that astonishes us. This is a shocking poetry, and the shock is not of recognition but of estrangement. It makes an unfamiliar claim upon us, the claim of apostasy. In such lines as these:

> I think of how the mystics read
> by the light of their own bodies.

What a world of darkness that must have been
to read by the flaming hearts
that turn into heaps of ash on the altar,
how everything in the end is made
equal by the wind.

we are exposed to a dangerous degree of radiation, an
energy everywhere active in this astonishing first book
not of poems, then, but of poetry, a poetry of what
Aldous Huxley once called downward and backward
Christian soldiers. Awe-struck, I salute Timothy Liu
on his desecrated battlefield.

RICHARD HOWARD

I

ARIEL SINGING

It is not happiness. Not the man standing
in line waiting to show me his poppies
and doves. Not a vase or an empty cage
he leaves when the magic act is over.
It is sleeping for a long time, the rest
of the world standing in a broken line.
Or waking without new flowers flaming
into this world. It is a world without song
I flew right into. In the glass I saw
one soul, not two colliding into one.
Nothing shattered. What is fragile came after,
time to kill. We love badly. Do you see
how we lie awake, always hungry in bed?
The priests continue to hold out their fast
offerings to the weak. Amen. Teach me
how to sing in a grove of olive trees,
to fall as a sparrow. It is all I want.

LABYRINTH

The yellow shirt of joy hangs
like a ghost in the moth-eaten
heart. I accept this absence,
this gift that has not fallen
apart in my hands. And all
those shirtless nights I loved

in another country, the harps
of angels crashing down stairs.
That music before all tension
ceased. Nothing sounded right again.
Except the tigers pacing behind
the walls, the click of claws.

THE TREE THAT KNOWLEDGE IS

I do not want to die. Not for love.
Nor a vision of that tree I cannot
recollect, shining in the darkness
with cherubim and a flaming sword.
All my life that still small voice
of God coiled up inside my body.
The lopped-off branch that guilt is
is not death. Nor life. But the lust
that flowers at the end of it.

PASSION

always red lopium

By mid-afternoon, all is imprecision:
the brittle poppies in the garden
      a bright suffusion of crimson and saffron
          the honey bees darting
      in and out of the miniature roses
beyond the topiary, two children
      in a maze of bronze trees reaching out
          to support the sky, their mother
      in a gallery on Rodeo Drive
walking among the Erté statues *— androgynous*
      turning the little price tags over
          an old man reciting Rumi
      in a bistro across the street
stirring a cup of double espresso
      contemplating the passion of Christ
          a musician in a Brooklyn flat
      burning down his studio
all the needles pushing red
      a lifetime of tape unravelling
          for ye have the poor with you always
      but me ye have not always
a child selling plastic roses
      tiny charges running through the stem
          I would love to kiss you
      the scent of women wrapped in mink
the price of kissing is your life
      lap dogs trailing behind on long leashes
          now my loving is running toward my life

shouting, one of woman, another of Christ:
a man with two tattoos on his biceps
      bashing a fag on Christopher Street
          what a bargain, let's buy it
      a statue wrapped in tissue paper
set inside a sturdy cardboard box
      noli me tangere
         a trick in Hollywood dying from AIDS
     making his way to the Avenue of the Stars
to sink his palms in pavement
      Eloi, Eloi, lama sabacthani
        the children home in time for supper.

7

THE CITY

Here rats are the totem animal
without a flower to offer
the table, our knives and forks
their enemies, which is why
we all go hungry. A bomber
flies overhead, my mother
calling and calling,
blind to the lovers singing
beneath cemetery trees
or the wild-eyed suicides
dancing in alleys with barrels
of shotguns in their mouths.

NEITHER MOTH NOR RUST

You see it was impossible.
Death was worse than all
the books my mother returned
on time. So the fines added up

till the day of her funeral.
Now the unexpected guests
arrive, poor as they are,
taking her crystal and china.

FROM XIAN

Incense fills the bazaar of crafted-jade
near Xian, where the black veiled hawkers squat
on concrete, selling lover's charms. Each lot
displays with pride its priceless trinkets made
in Hong Kong: bracelets from antiquity,
hoops carved from elephant tusks, worn
at court by ladies wrapped in silk, engaging sport
for desperate men, a fallen dynasty.
Such quiet scenes are frozen in relief
around your delicate wrist, bone on bone,
the splendor of our love an imitation
of ages past. Protect it well: belief
outlasts the grave, those foreign walls of stone
where we bartered in the underground station.

★

How years can change a face: fracture lines
down terracotta figurines deface
their pristine image, though delinquent grace
survives the sculptor's hands. To him, the signs
of wear were visible, where time has drained
the lips of color, worn the delicate
eyelids smooth, the inner life celibate
in glory of its maker. They have reigned
for centuries with broken hands and feet,
their crumbled sex, the yin and yang laid low
in the dust of Xian. But how we wake
from beds of darkness. Patiently we eat
the silent space of years, longing to know
what will remain when light begins to break.

Across dry oceans of winter I'll come
to lie with you beneath the village trees
and talk of spring: cherry blossoms and bees
swirling in winds of cold delirium
on the outskirts of Xian. The steaming
bowls of congee will ruddy our faces
where years have worn away lover's graces.
You told me how fruit would follow the sting
while peeling the thousand-year egg, then set
those pellucid slices of jade with care
on the china between us. So swiftly
my chopsticks flew up like a stork, a wet
fish in its beak, tears frozen in the air
of the fan you folded into the sea.

*

The women are weaving baskets with straw
they've gathered by the village stream flowing
down to ruined cities. Their hands, slowing
with age, will work designs that bear no flaw,
binding the flax of youth with mortal thread
they've spun for generations. Take my hand
that shows no mark of age, and let the sand
along these shores fall through, into that bed
where we must rest. The greatness of their past
shall be no more than tender straw made strong
to hold the bread they harvest from their fields
where ten thousand soldiers of clay outlast
the wars their kingdoms fought, their bloodless song
arising from corroded swords and shields.

AWAITING TRANSLATION

My habit is reading only beginnings
of books in a stranger's tongue, or else
      waiting for a new translation, the meaning
           of lines still imprisoned on the shelf.
    To set myself free! So often I have missed
the chance to dive into an ocean
      of imported words (not that I'd resist
           the drowning), yet I've felt the motion
    of the wind-tossed water slowly taking me
farther and farther out in its tides . . .
    If only I could balance that cardboard sea
           on the crown of my head, I would try
    dousing it with fire, that hard-cover cross
(no heavier than a human heart).
    The ink and paper would save me, not because
           words can save any more than the Ark
    or the City of Enoch (all saved in the Bible)
but because words must come to an end.
    Did Columbus know there'd be an end to all
           his travels — did he expect to find
    a new world? Picture him washed up on a shelf
of sand, blazing forth again! I wish
    I could be like him and somehow keep myself
           alive, leave the last word unfinished.

THE OTHER LANGUAGE

Nothing on the pages
can articulate what we did
not trust. Last night, a dog
with your face spoke to me.
My eyes were closed,
the heavy balls of dreams
sliding back and forth
in their separate cells
like synchronized swimmers,
each tacit movement a gift
we did not share, that dog
talking in a language
that does not belong to us.

PATIENCE

I sit in the square, listening
to the beggar's cup filling
with gold teeth. A woman kneels
at the curb, cleaning a virgin
she has kissed into brownness
while her children dig up forks
from a window box.
                    All morning,
not a bird has landed near
the seeds I have scattered
on these stones. Only laughter
in the distance where young men
walking in threes vanish behind
an olive grove.
                    A flutter of wings
and the world is finished.

HIS BODY LIKE CHRIST PASSED
IN AND OUT OF MY LIFE

A woman selling Bibles at the Greyhound station.
Me waiting. I was not indifferent, only hardened.
A German violin instead of her voice. Headphones
in my ears. The smell of that place, diesel and Brahms.
Me waiting as others wait. Me turning the cassette,
she turning pages in that purgatory without deliverance.
Later my lover smiling as Jesus, always late, never
his fault. Me looking back at a woman praising God.
Her devotion. My envy. A desire for permanence.
For a world without betrayal. I think of that winter,
the tracks outside my window erased from a field
of snow, me ironing sheets as if no one had slept
there. A bus heading South without me. My car
not starting, dead batteries, an empty walkman
discarded under the bed. How the world slides away.
Me diminished by the thought of him. Of spring.
What are birds returning, singing, compared to this,
the lives that I have forsaken to honor a god.

WHITE STONE

To him who conquers I will give some of the hidden manna, and I will give him a white stone, with a new name written on the stone which no one knows except him who receives it.

Revelation 2:17

He used the third person to avoid
    intimacy, refusing to speak his name
        in the presence of the elders, taking

the host into his mouth for sins he had
    not yet committed. He painted angels
        on the bathroom ceiling, rejecting

the trinity as love. It was only
    an instance, a gold-plated crucifix
        the size of a charm on a boy's bracelet:

a cross hanging on a body, a body
    hanging on a cross—this was the image
        he couldn't stop. Surely it was an act

of devotion hailing Mary, God, the Christ-
    child, all spinning into existence,
        not so much dancing as flying apart

in a universe endlessly expanding.
    Chairs without arms or legs were carried
        into the chapel as the brides moved up

the aisle, suckling infants in the folds
    of their gowns, rejecting him for another
        groom: *though a mother can have two sons,*

a son can never have two mothers. Yet
        he attended every wedding, knelt down
                to the grains of rice he had garnered

in a bell jar. The addiction became
        unbearable, a death like many deaths
                collecting holy relics left behind:

lipstick-stained statuettes, shattered vials
        of olive oil. His whole life he had craved
                for an audience to watch him dance across

the trapdoors of their praise. Not that applause
        mattered. Nor an encore. For these were mere
                repetitions, a shower to wash away

the sweat, the cosmetic glow from his face.
        So he drew a star on his door and slept
                with multiple partners, each man holding

a white stone that embraced an entire
        history. This was the sign, a language
                to translate the world into a sea of glass,

a gift God had given those who had
        survived *the holy baptism of fire*,
                the ceiling of their art collapsing

to reveal another heaven. He could
    not escape this vision. Closing his eyes,
        he found himself in a black car, driving

without a steering wheel down a tree-lined
    road. Beside him rode a bicycle from
        his childhood, a tiny bell ringing through

the air. *No hands* he heard himself say
    as he swerved into a ditch. There he knelt
        and saw the birth of beauty. With his bare

hands, he dug a modest grave, lined it
    with leaves from a branch within his reach.
        There, unfolding a silk handkerchief

monogrammed with a stranger's name, he tossed
    that stone in the grave, and with a deft stroke
        wiped his forehead clean.

WALKING IN A WORLD WHERE WE ARE SOMETIMES LOVED

A wind blows news the sunlight
has yellowed across the street.
We walk into a forest
            and are lost. Either our cries
are heard or we bury ourselves
without God. This morning
            was no different: new leaves
            on the ground, a storm pouring
in through windows of that room
where we made love, thundering
            doves flying out of our mouths.

VOX ANGELICA

I sing to a breeze that runs through the rafters.
A woman skins a snake. She turns
but not enough for me to see her face.
In the sink, the peelings have begun to pile up
in a mound the color of dirt.
She hears the oil hissing on its own
and thinks of throwing something in—
ginger, garlic, chopped rings of green onion—
but doesn't, lets the oil brown
until the smoke rises
and fills the dark corners of the kitchen.
The birds tonight are louder than ever
perched beside a river of flying fish.

*

The sweat on her feverish face
dissipates, flying upward
to God as she clings to the shoulders
of death, her feet touching
neither heaven nor earth.
They say death has a nobility of its own
but all she could hear was weeping—
not entirely a human sound
but a sound as if made by a machine
that played again and again
like a tape she could not erase.
She tried to explain the sadness,
the leaves changing to a color
she could no longer describe.

*

The hour of the Bible is dead.
Neither dirt nor flowers
can keep her body warm enough.
Driving from the service,
I keep my hands on the wheel
as if steadying myself
the way silence holds each word in place.
I imagine lying down next to her
as earth is sprinkled over our eyes,
our mouths filling with dirt.

⋆

The angels are singing
in the shadows of the house,
night a black cat sitting on my chest,
claws extended toward my face,
the scar on my body
a witness to that place where the world
had once been opened, muscle
and blood. How a vision
pinned me down until my scream
reached two worlds
on both sides of the glass.
Everything happened twice
in the cat's eyes,
the slow engine of happiness
seducing me back to sleep.

⋆

The words I speak I cannot revise.
All art is an afterthought,
an attempt to interpret a dream
that by its nature is perfected,
the bed unmade, and me almost late
to my next appointment where more of me
must get cut out. The horror
of getting beyond the skin,
the small white aberration that I dreamed
would not grow back, not enlarge
to fill my entire conscious body.
I think of how the mystics read
by the light of their own bodies.
What a world of darkness that must have been
to read by the flaming hearts
that turn into heaps of ash on the altar,
how everything in the end is made
equal by the wind.

II

(mother)

MAMA

If I had known this burden on my tongue,
would I have refused the first syllable
she taught me in the garden? *Ma. Ma.*
It would take me years to make any new
distinctions: *milk, truck, book, clock,*
facets to a glass house I was trapped
inside, until one day, that great stone
of marriage fell from my mother's hand.
Such freedom gave me grief to visit
her poorly lit efficiency across town,
the streets I had to name in order
to get there: *Dogwood, Cherry, Orchard Creek.*
It grew more difficult. She moved twice
in a week before the county moved her
behind buzzered doors and wired glass
where a sign still hangs: *Closed Community.*
Good Sam hospital was too new for maps.
A voice on the other end of the line,
impersonal as God, helped me get there
before explaining how an unnamed man
went down from Jerusalem to Jericho
and fell among thieves who wounded him,
leaving him half-dead, how a priest and Levite
spat on him while a certain Samaritan
dressed the open wounds with oil and wine,
gave up his own beast and left two pence
for the host at the inn. I marvelled
at such buildings named after the nameless,

how as a college freshman, I sat in Franz Hall,
understood at last what Mother said to me,
her *poverty of content*, a kind of *word salad*:
I dreamed he had folded six times. Jesus
said the sheep he called would make one fold.
I thought at the time the Latin for six
is sex, that the number of the beast is 666.
Is sex then beastly? All people have eyes.
These blind people are led about by a boy.
One can hear too much. It took me years to turn
from Adler, Skinner and Freud back to the Good
Samaritan's words: *whatsoever thou spendest*
more, when I come again, I will repay thee.
Mama, the debt incurred from just one word.
Locked up for twenty years, only syllables now
for what we left unspoken: *rage, shame, guilt,*
everything you taught me from the start.

SHE SINGS IN ALL
HER SEASONS

To see her for what she is.
Reclined and unadorned.
The flowers on the table
in no set arrangement,
a white dress lilting
in the open window.
This is what I love:
how she wears the seasons
so life will come to her.
Her open mouth. Longing
in the shape of desire,
a boat without oars
at the dead center
of a lake. The sun
that moves within her
as the air catches fire.
A lightness I delight in.
Her heaviness: the flowers
spilling from her hair.

THE KORE

What was sacred was in my journey
the whole way back, leaving her
in pieces the way I had found her.

APHRODITE AS I KNOW HER

It is not ruin but the tenderness
I love. Not what time destroys
but what remains: the empty
hands broken off at the wrists.
How can I tell you what I know
of Aphrodite, how I found her
weeping at the gates of the city
or kneeling by the river at night,
without diminishing her love for me?
Who is now inside me singing.
Who continues to efface herself
in spite of me. Destroy her
temple and who will raise me up?
Not the sibyls dragging away
the broken columns, the tokens
of that life they most desired.

THE GATES OF HELL

All morning they were lining up to eat.
Neither they nor the food was ready.
Nothing was prepared. Except the dog,
his tongue hanging down from his mouth,
who followed each soul like a shadow.

INDIAN SUMMER

That summer, Charlie drew a cunt
with a black crayon, taught me
how to lick the alphabet.
My mother almost caught us
in her drawers, putting on
the panties and gowns. He slept
in my bed every night after
his parents split. He taught me
how to trust my pouty lips
wrapped around his hairless cock,
tongue sliding arcross his crack
the way I sealed my letters home
while away at camp. That summer
we rode each other like horses,
fearing Indians in the bushes
along the edge of a bluff.
Then it was over. We cried
at the airport. He promised me
postcards from another world.
When school started again,
I wanted to show him all
the stamps that I had mounted.

PORNOGRAPHY

There was something appalling about that
body, the delicate crease across
the skin, the hair falling off
the illuminated shoulders no thinner
than my mother's the day I saw her
taking a shower, the disarming beads
of water trickling down to her dark v.
The newness in the power of my hands
undressing the women willingly.
I felt that strange excitement of guilt,
of not desiring them, dancers lifted
straight up in the air, scissor-kicked
legs suspended over my head. Mostly
I was afraid of my neurotic mother:
*Sit down when you pee! I will not wipe
a stained seat.* Once we saw Baryshnikov
doing jétes across a page, that bulge
going hard in my crotch, eyes fixed
on his form, his muscles a rippling flag
from a land I had longed to know. Later
I would thumb through *People* and *Time*,
a *Playgirl* wedged between the covers.
The life that I could not own I stole,
better than Baryshnikov, the men
who taught me how to dance the hard way.
I dreamed I was lost in Baryshnikov's
closet, his many costumes hanging there
like ghosts that he no longer had to play,

the ballerinas all turning in his mind
like silver mobiles, glitter falling
from their wands, his arms extended
toward that corner where I crouched. Naked,
I slipped into the body of a woman,
a white plume of feathers snaking around
our legs, the pas de deux of our hearts
leaping clouds stiff as laundry, arabesque
of moonlight across the city's concrete
skyline where hundreds of men below
continued to pose in the glossy pages I had
stashed beneath my mattress, a prince's
hidden pea having kept me up all night
I thought I would never come down again.

SEX

Her dress was the color of lemons
just before harvest. *Help me*, I said.
She said, *you take what you can get.*
It was then a young man carrying tea
entered the room with a smile, knowing
what would happen next. How the book
at the touch of his fingertips
ignited like a scrap of flash paper
from the magic set my father gave me
for my birthday. My favorite trick
was pushing that pencil through a photo
encased in glass, pulling red ribbons
through the hole, then sliding out
the image restored. After one or two
shows, I locked myself in a closet.
What memories in an instant of burning,
like a chain of knotted silks pulled out
from a child's mouth, then gathered
in those hands that released a dove
across a dim sea of faces where I sat.
Where did those wings of illusion
come to rest after the show was over?
A room full of empty chairs, only a cup
of cold tea with dragons swimming
through the clouds of their own breath
remained on stage, where I had longed
to stand before the tea evaporated.
Drink, he said, tears on his face,
sliced lemons engraved on the kettle.

CONSOLATION

Don't want to go out. The toilet
growing dark with mold. Wax fruit
on a plate. Have learned to keep
things simple. Nothing I cannot fix.
My hair. A button. Whatever helps

me sleep. A slow drip from the tap.
Something constant. Clear. Not
wanting to strike a match. Or make
decisions. The weight of my head
in my hands, old linen on the table.

A ROOM WITHOUT DOORS

At the end of the maze, a mouse
was swallowed whole, backed against glass.
    I was fascinated by the snake
        shedding its skin, that diamond exigence.
    Even snakes on our black and white
forced my mother to leave the room,
    that close-up of the head, venom
        being milked into a shatterproof
    beaker. *Different marks distinguish
king from coral, male from female.*
    I gave up cartoons, took a weekend
        class just to get out of that house.
    Later near a sewer, I found a rubber
snake. Mother would not touch it
    though it turned up everywhere—
        the icebox, pantry, under her pillow.
    And her therapist couldn't help
but offer her reassurance, a kind
    of gestalt malpractice, fingers
        pointing to his crotch: *I feel tension
here. Come here.* It happened
so swiftly, my mother in a mental
    ward, a therapist walking off
        with her mink coat. It is after
    the video where a woman
sleeps in the corner of a room,
    mice safe in their cages for another
        night, a big screen turning to snow.

SEPARATION

After the first loss, there is no other,
the rest is repetition: first grade to second,
second to third, from desk to desk without
my mother. One day I couldn't, and the next
I could—tie shoes, tell time, write words—
lessons I can't give back: my mother and father
leaving each other, the house going up for sale,
me sweating over a breakfast grill, flipping
hotcakes to put myself through school that first
year in the dorms. So free we were it seemed
without our histories, as if *we* could leave
and start again, our lives undone by a distant
grace. From East to West, Nanking to New York,
how my parents collided in Washington Square,
then drove across the Rockies to a starter
home where I was born. *Ten thousand rooms
from birth to death*, Glen used to say, after
a couple of hits, before he gassed himself
in his parents' car while they were in Bermuda.
I remember the book my mother gave me, people
disappearing into that Devil's Triangle,
entire planes. The black and white photos
caught my eye, a kind of proof. I never saw him
again, only heard about exhaust and a garden
hose. They found him naked, a note in his hand
no one could understand. How rooms are emptied
by a single act. All through school I had a dream
of roll being called and I not being there.
Everything rises up again, not like the stars

climbing into heaven, but to that place I keep
returning to late at night, a light, a desk,
a chair, no different from what my parents have
owned, knowing how this would be the poem
that I would write for the rest of my life.

CANKER

The wound would not heal for days. But that was nothing compared to my mother who ran her mouth all over my body.

What people will do to be remembered.

The nurses cutting roses from the cards I sent have put them in a tub of scalding water. The kisses have come undone.

Stamps are all she can save, arranging them in a book like the photographs she could never take.

I have managed to piece together the pages she tore away from me. Though the box of letters burned, the ashes were not entirely extinguished.

The day after Christmas break, my father was driving me back to school, the two-lane highway on fire, everything falling.

To me their divorce was never final, only a precarious extension, a bridge I had learned to walk between two cliffs.

Of course we had a great distance to go, taking our turns at the wheel. My father never had a steady foot, only a start–stop rhythm that burned more gas than I thought we would have before reaching

the next station. But we would make it. It was belief that kept us at each other's throats.

I remember blood on the dining room floor and a few drops down his cheek when I broke a chair over his back. It wasn't damaged beyond repair, but it was put away in the attic.

And I thought, if only Mother knew. The county had already locked her up for the first time that year: her neighbors had complained about sacks of garbage she threw from her balcony into the swimming pool below.

I still can hear her voice that day in junior high when I was called out of class. She said to me in the backseat,

Love me, let me die,

her head bobbing in my lap, floating in its pool of chemicals. The woman who couldn't get in to clean drove us to the emergency room.

Let me die.

That's all I heard when I broke into her bedroom, the pills scattered on the floor like a broken necklace.

She lived. That night there was a canker in the back of my throat. I couldn't eat for days. My father opened cans of a protein drink he'd brought home from the hospital.

Drink this. Now sleep. Good.

That was the first time I remember being held. I told my father at the end of our trip. I told him about the men who came into my life. The pain that made me feel alive.

My father wept as we swerved to the side of the road. Then he began to speak, stoking a bed of ashes that years could not put out:

Your aunt wrote me while you had stayed with them, still a baby. You'd scream if your mother came into the room where you were being bathed. Her sister told her not to touch you but she did.

I wanted this to stop. Why couldn't anyone stop her?

There are no photographs of you then. She wouldn't have them in the house reminding her.

My mother entered me with a kiss.

At Easter break, I flew on a half-empty plane into the eye of night. I didn't bring her flowers, though I thought of how they would look on a grave.

I wanted her in the earth, her body contained.

Not floating down a river of fire. Not knowing the words she said to me that night would burn:

Your father lies. Please God, don't hurt your mother. You were always so difficult, crying, crying. I couldn't shut you up. You didn't want my milk. Only your father. How could I live with myself?

After we cried, I put out the light. I left her in that room. I closed the door behind me.

Tonight my roses bloom beside her bed, working their thorns into her lips, the words I never knew how to say:

Mother, nothing heals completely as long as I stay alive.

III

EROS APTEROS

The wings are no longer there
to lift this god out of time.

I have come to be healed, reaching
around the marble sides to hold
what remains, resting my chin
on a stump where the head
has been.
                    Limbs severed
above the elbows, below the hips
its mutilated sex, testicles
hanging in a stone sack.

The oil and sweat on my hands
continue to hurt this body
beyond feeling.
                    Such guilt
to run my finger down the spine,
along that road winding back
two thousand years, this touching
the proof that I am here.

THE STORM

A dark wing lifting my umbrella.
The birds oppress me,
                singing
in spite of the rain that falls
through ravished leaves,
                  the moon
diminished, sailing over trees
like a sad note.
              Why this barbaric
din of beak and claw gripping
broken branches,
                the mind's skin
stretched across black spokes
rooted to my hand.

ON A HILL AT NIGHT
IN A CHAIR UNDER STARS

A face at the window. Doves
floating down from the eaves.
He drifting off. No stars.
A parliament of owls roosting
in the branches. By morning
there were flowers everywhere.

THE HEAT

So he hung himself
in the walk-in closet with a styrofoam head
without a wig or scarf to make it look
more human. Like a hook of meat swinging inside
a deli locker or live bait dangling
through ceilings of ice is how he felt when he saw
his lover rolled away, eyes fixed on that
metal cart. For days he hid behind sunglasses
and a wig, reading obituaries
beneath the live oak, a child walking a dog
through beds of impatiens so brilliant
he thought he too was suffocating, his bare feet
grounded in that heat.

LEAVING THE UNIVERSE

Can't go back
to his body. That wilderness.
A time he would let me
rest there, no other place to go.
A bedroom
full of star charts, planets tearing
free from orbit, a belt
of asteroids flying apart.
In that space
between us, the gravity
of my bed unable
to keep his body from floating
out the door.

CARCASS

I can smell it now,
your cheap sex up my ass,
your eyes stuck in my back
like Chinese stars. Pull out.
You can still make it
to the border on a half-tank
if you don't stop
for the sirens flashing
in your rearview mirror.
I'll be close behind you.
Feel my black wings
buckle like beautiful knees
going down on dead meat.

9 1 1

We met as blind men, trying to see
ourselves, groping for words
to suggest an image — *a doctor,*
a lawyer, a student — anything that
we weren't. Yet he did most
of the talking: *where you from*
and what do you like to do?
When lust transmits its own disease,
it overtakes the body faster
than an ambulance pushing its way
through the crowded streets.
The distance grew as darkness
stretched across our voices shot
through miles of glass nerves,
a taste of black between our teeth:
don't hang up — what's your name? —
talk to me — you into French? — Greek? —
German? — Top? — Bottom? — First time? —
Relax. I did what he told me to do.
I knew I was safe. *Harder.* I knew
I was alone. *That's it.* I knew I
would never have to listen to him
again. *Keep it coming. Want it all.*
No one could break our connection,
a spiral cord wrapped around my neck,
inches burning against my aching
wrist as I held on to the white
circumference of his perfect waist.

SFO/HIV/JFK

I knew his job was more than cleaning up
the men's room, waiting for the next man to come
to the polished seat he shined with his spit.
Call it my lucky day, my flight touching
down on an icy runway, wheels skidding
into the unmarked safety of a warm
terminal. I dropped my pants straight off
that long connecting flight to a city
I'd never know, except in passing through.
His city. He showed me pictures: a wife
he met in high school, two sons who attend.
He showed me this in an office downstairs,
having caught my attention with his flashing
pen, toilet paper scrolled up onto it,
had scrawled *I like to suck, get sucked, and fuck.*
If your mother tells you love is decent,
don't believe her, until she tells the truth.
Understand me when I say I didn't
do it for sex. I did it for pity.
For the hundreds of men that I have loved
in airports, busstops, truckstops, interstate
reststops, shopping malls, locker rooms
and janitorial closets, wherever there's enough
room for two men to stand up face to face.
Don't ask me what it's like to go on
living, at first a high priest breaking bread
for hundreds of open mouths, finally
feeding myself in some airport snack bar,
smell of a stranger's sex on my fingers.

SODOM AND GOMORRAH

No other world than this.
When I close my eyes, cities

burn. The men I cannot touch
I name. When strangers knock,

death gathers at the door
and flies out of our mouths,

that swan song in our throats
a falling cloud of ash.

VOLUNTEERS AT
THE AIDS FOUNDATION

They asked us to close our eyes, said this
was the end of our training. On the floor
entranced, our bodies
                    released their breath —
asked us to imagine a door, another, another,
each an unfamiliar lover, the last one
disinfected,
                the clinic I entered alone.
Picture a chart that's marked with a number
while someone in a lab coat looks at you,
breaking the tip of a pencil.
                        As you leave
with a number of someone else to reach, think
of those who'll know the result of your test
that's just beginning.
                    In a dizzying lot,
you cannot find your car. Consider the make
of every car you ever rode in, every face
behind each wheel . . .
                    your friends have come
with flowers in fluted vases, leaving words
you cannot read, so many syringes. You think
of children near the tide
                        letting go
of bright balloons when you're too far gone
to care for those who remain in the flesh
weeping with the staff.

LAST CHRISTMAS

We often made angels on your lawn,
watching the bodies fade a little more
each day, until the wings were gone.

Traditions die hard. We had enough
for the "family" recipe: cognac, cream,
a dozen eggs, a box of nutmeg, spice

for garnish. *It was Christ who drank
the bitter cup. Loving all men,
he gave up his life*, you sang.

To the left of your smile, that patch
of KS like a dark flower bloomed
in a field of snow. Yet no one came

to visit. This Christmas at your grave,
no flowers, but maybe a cup of eggnog,
a sprinkle of nutmeg on the snow.

THE QUILT

These are my lovers

        whose patches of color fade,
whose stitches have run

        wild in their patterns
of grief: the men who die

        and die in each other's arms,
leaving us their names.

        Together, we begin to see
the future's design,

        each square bleeding
into the next, our voices

        a fallen choir. Each day
the quilt spreads out

        more rapidly, covering
the earth's four corners.

        Who can sleep tonight
when beds are soaked

        with sweat, when bodies
are being sponged away

            by nurses who know
the cost? When desire

            has crumbled into that sea
rising in our chests,

            the last breath floating
down the river, consider

            death without judgement
and let each spool of thread

            unravel its plot of pain:
in *A Tale of Two Cities,*

            the woman knitting life
and death together

            never saw herself consumed
by her passion. That story

            has not changed, but we will
go on loving, embracing

            our own grief, our lives
split open like a book

            where the names are written.

MORE THAN HALF THE LEAVES
ALREADY DOWN

Dragging that plastic sheet across the lawn
like a canoe filled with the season's last
leaves (mostly from the maple, all standing
flame in the center of your yard) is how
we managed to clear away the summer,
making a waist-high bed under birches
near the property line. It was nothing
that I had imagined, such romantic
foreplay, layer after layer lifted
into our arms, all those wounded colors
from a world in transition soon to be
dumped. In that sky the leaves still falling —
no chore to sing out in such choirs.
This was joy, gathering in the corners
of that tarp the size of a fishing net
we pulled against the ground's green current.
Later we would row on actual water
the color of steel, beyond the reach
of an inconsolable music, each leaf
spiraling down that cold declivity
toward gravity's sudden tenderness.
This was the dance I had always wanted,
the two of us in that stillness, nowhere
near shore, with work ahead of us, and yet
each stroke suspended, red-tailed hawks soaring
overhead, our bodies leaning into silence
like a pair of rakes left out by the tree.

POETRY FROM ALICE JAMES BOOKS

The Calling (Tom Absher) Thirsty Day (Kathleen Aguero) In the Mother Tongue (Catherine Anderson) Backtalk (Robin Becker) Personal Effects (Becker, Minton, Zuckerman) Legacies (Suzanne Berger) Disciplining the Devil's Country (Carole Borges) Afterwards; Letters from an Outlying Province (Patricia Cumming) Riding with the Fireworks (Ann Darr) Chemo-Poet and Other Poems (Helene Davis) Children of the Air (Theodore Deppe) ThreeSome Poems (Dobbs, Gensler, Knies) The Forked Rivers (Nancy Donegan) 33; US:Women (Marjorie Fletcher) No One Took a Country from Me (Jaqueline Frank) Forms of Conversion (Allison Funk) Natural Affinities (Erica Funkhouser) Rush to the Lake (Forrest Gander) Without Roof (Kinereth Gensler) Bonfire (Celia Gilbert) Permanent Wave; Signal::Noise (Miriam Goodman) To the Left of the Worshipper (Jeffrey Greene) Romance and Capitalism at the Movies (Joan Joffe Hall) Raw Honey (Marie Harris) Making the House Fall Down (Beatrice Hawley) The Old Chore (John Hildebidle) Impossible Dreams (Pati Hall) Robeson Street (Fanny Howe) The Chicago Home (Linnea Johnson) The Knot (Alice Jones) From Room to Room (Jane Kenyon) Streets After Rain (Elizabeth Knies) Sleep Handbook; The Secretary Parables (Nancy Lagomarsino) Dreaming in Color (Ruth Lepson) Falling Off the Roof (Karen Lindsey) Vox Angelica (Timothy Liu) Temper; Black Dog (Margo Lockwood) Rosetree (Sabra Loomis) Shrunken Planets (Robert Louthan) Sea Level (Suzanne Matson) Animals (Alice Mattison) The Common Life (David McKain) The Canal Bed (Helena Minton) Your Skin Is a Country (Nora Mitchell) Openers; French for Soldiers (Nina Nyhart) Night Watches: Inventions on the Life of Maria Mitchell (Carole Oles) Wolf Moon; Pride & Splendor (Joan Pedrick) The Hardness Scale (Joyce Peseroff) Before We Were Born (Carol Potter) Lines Out (Rosamond Rosenmeir) Curses; The Country Changes (Lee Rudolph) Box Poems (Willa Schneberg) Against That Time; Moving to a New Place (Ron Schreiber) Contending with the Dark (Jeffrey Schwartz) Changing Faces; Appalachian Winter; Rooms Overhead (Betsy Scholl) From This Distance (Susan Snively) Deception Pass (Sue Standing) Infrequent Mysteries (Pamela Stewart) Blue Holes (Laurel Trivelpiece) Home Deep Blue: New & Selected Poems; The River at Wolfe (Jean Valentine) Trans-Siberian Railway; Green Shaded Lamps (Cornelia Veenendaal) Old Sheets (Larkin Warren) Tamsen Donner: a Woman's Journey; Permanent Address (Ruth Whitman)